Best Bible STORIES

INSIDE A FISH

Jennifer Rees Larcombe
Illustrated by Steve Björkman

Marshall Pickering
An Imprint of HarperCollins*Publishers*

Marshall Pickering is an Imprint of
HarperCollins*Religious*
Part of HarperCollins*Publishers*
77–85 Fulham Palace Road,
London W6 8JB
www.christian-publishing.co.uk

First published in 1992 in Great Britain
by Marshall Pickering as part of the
Children's Bible Story Book by Jennifer Rees Larcombe
This edition published in 2000 by Marshall Pickering

1 3 5 7 9 10 8 6 4 2

A catalogue record for this book is
available from the British Library.

ISBN 0 551 03247 2

Printed and bound in Hong Kong

INSIDE A FISH

'But God! The Assyrians are dreadful people! Surely you don't love them?' spluttered the prophet Jonah in disgust. 'I do,' replied God. 'Go to their wicked city Nineveh and tell them

if they don't change their ways I will have to destroy them all.'

‘I’m **not** doing that!’ thought Jonah crossly.
‘They’re our enemies;

I want them **destroyed!’**

So instead of crossing the desert to Nineveh, as God had told him, he jumped on to a ship going in quite the **opposite** direction. He was forgetting that

you can't run away from God; He is everywhere.

'I'll soon be safe in Spain,' he thought as he fell happily to sleep. But when he woke a dreadful storm had hit the ship. It creaked and groaned as the huge waves crashed over the decks and the wind screamed round the mast.

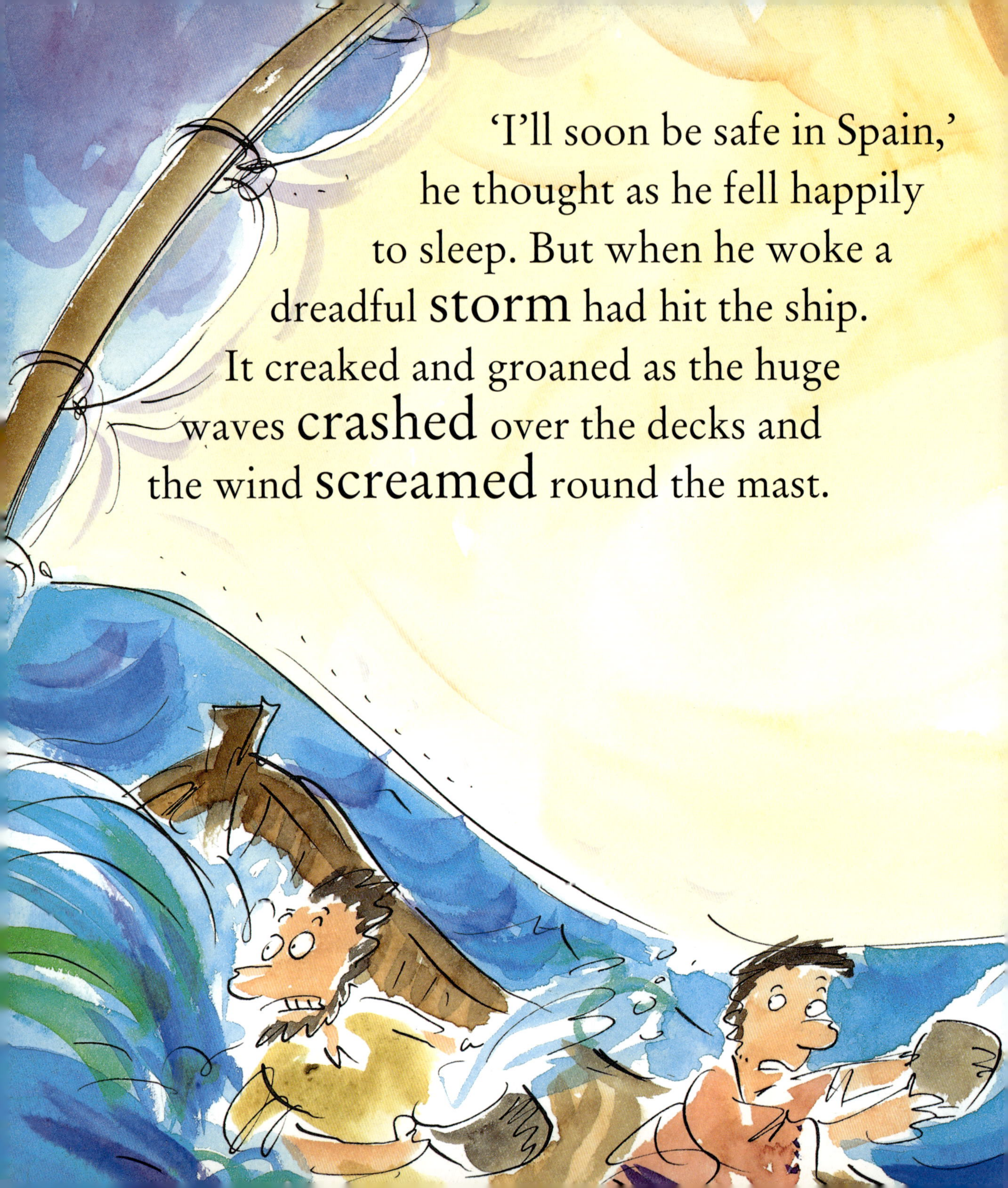

'We're
going to
sink!'

cried the sailors.

'God must be **angry** with me,' thought Jonah, 'because I disobeyed Him.'

'Throw me **overboard,'**

he shouted to the captain.

'This storm is **all** my fault.'

Down and down sank Jonah, under the raging waves. Salt water **choked** him and seaweed **tangled** round his head.

'I'm going to die,' he thought.
But God had already planned for a
great fish to swim along and swallow
him just in time. It's not much fun inside a
fish's tummy –
very dark and smelly.

But as soon as Jonah told God how very
sorry he was, the fish swam ashore
and was very sick on the beach.
'Now off you go to Nineveh,' said God.
'Oh no!' grumbled Jonah, but this time
he did not dare to disobey.

‘In forty days’ time God will
wipe you all away,’
he shouted above the noise of Nineveh’s busy streets. Crowds gathered round him and soon they began to **cry.**

When the King heard what Jonah was saying, he climbed down from his golden throne and, taking off his fine robes,

he covered himself in a dirty old sack. 'No one in the city must eat or drink,' he ordered.

'Everyone must pray

that God will

forgive us.'

As soon as God heard their prayers and saw how sorry they all were,

He changed his mind

and decided **not** to destroy the city after all. Jonah was cross. 'I knew this would happen,' he grumbled.

'God is **just too kind**.

These dreadful people deserved to die.'

Angrily he left Nineveh and climbed a **high** hill nearby, still hoping to see the city **burnt to the ground**. But of course nothing happened.

The sun beat down on him and gave him a headache. He felt sick, thirsty, and crosser than ever. 'I wish I was dead,' he thought.
'This is worse than the fish's tummy.'

'Why are you so angry with me?'
God's voice made Jonah jump.
'I made all those people down in that city, just as I made you.' Jonah sat and thought about that for a long time; then he walked all the way home and wrote this story down in a book.

'Now,' he thought,

'people all over the world will know

just how much God loves us all.'

Jonah 1 – 4